Basketball

• An Introduction to Being a Good Sport •

by Aaron Derr
illustrations by Scott Angle

RED CHAIR ·PRESS·

Start Smart books are published by Red Chair Press

Red Chair Press LLC   PO Box 333   South Egremont, MA 01258-0333
www.redchairpress.com

Publisher's Cataloging-In-Publication Data

Names: Derr, Aaron. | Angle, Scott, illustrator.

Title: Basketball : an introduction to being a good sport / by Aaron Derr ; illustrations by
    Scott Angle.

Description: South Egremont, MA : Red Chair Press, [2017] | Start smart: sports | Interest age
    level: 005-009. | Includes Fast Fact sidebars, a glossary and references for additional reading.
    | Includes bibliographical references and index. | Summary: "Playing a sport is good
    exercise and fun, but being part of a team is more fun for everyone when you know the rules
    of the game and how to be a good sport. Basketball is one of the most popular team sports
    around the world. In this book, readers learn the history of the game and the role of various
    positions on the court."-- Provided by publisher.

Identifiers: LCCN 2016934114 | ISBN 978-1-63440-130-2 (library hardcover) |
    ISBN 978-1-63440-136-4 (paperback) | ISBN 978-1-63440-142-5 (ebook)

Subjects: LCSH: Basketball--Juvenile literature. | Sportsmanship--Juvenile literature.
    CYAC: Basketball. | Sportsmanship.

Classification: LCC GV885.1 .D47 2017 (print) | LCC GV885.1 (ebook) | DDC 796.323--dc23

Illustration credits: Scott Angle; technical charts by Joe LeMonnier

Photo credits: Cover p. 5, 7, 11, 15, 17, 21, 22, 25, 27, 28, 30: Dreamstime; p. 32: Courtesy of the
author, Aaron Derr

This series first published by:
Red Chair Press LLC   PO Box 333   South Egremont, MA 01258-0333

Printed in the United States of America

Distributed in the U.S. by Lerner Publisher Services. www.lernerbooks.com

1116 1P CGBS17

Table of Contents

Words in **bold type** are defined
in the glossary.

CHAPTER 1

The Perfect Team

Brianna, Jayden and Nathan are best friends. But they could not be more different.

Brianna is short and skinny for her age. But she can really fun fast! Jayden isn't as fast as Brianna, but he is a little bit taller. And though Nathan might be the slowest, he is also the tallest and strongest of all three friends.

When Brianna is by herself, she can't reach high enough to get her three schoolbooks off the top shelf in her room. If Jayden is there, he can reach the top shelf, but he can't carry all three books at once.

If Nathan is there, he can carry more books than anybody, but he isn't even fast enough to catch his dog when it gets off its leash! That's why they all need each other. And that's what makes them so good at basketball.

THE BIG BASKETBALL BOOK

FUN FACT

Basketball was invented by a college gym teacher named James Naismith way back in 1891!

CHAPTER 2

The Big Game

Brianna plays **guard** for the Titans. She is one of the smallest players on the **court**, but that's okay, because Brianna is fast!

Jayden plays **forward** for the Titans. He is the perfect size for it. Not too small and not too big.

Nathan plays **center**. He is one of the tallest kids in school. And he's just the right size to help his team.

In basketball, you need some players who are big and tall, some players who are small and quick, and some players in between!

The Titans are facing their biggest challenge of the season in their last game. They're playing against the Bulldogs. The Bulldogs have already beaten them once before.

Brianna, Jayden and Nathan don't want to lose to that team again. They know they are going to have to try their best if they're going to have a chance to win.

DID YOU KNOW?

The first game of basketball was played in Springfield, Massachusetts, in December 1891. The players used a soccer ball, and instead of shooting the ball through nets, they used peach baskets. That's why they called it basketball. After every made basket, somebody had to climb up a ladder and get the ball! Eventually someone had the bright idea to remove the bottom of the peach baskets so the ball would fall right through.

To be good at basketball, you have to do more than just **make baskets**. You also have to make good passes to your **teammates**, and you have to play defense to stop the other team from scoring.

You have to run as fast as you can, and you have to pay attention all the time. You never know when the ball is going to come to you!

Against the Bulldogs, Brianna, Jayden, Nathan and all of their teammates have to be at the top of their game.

JUST JOKING!

Q: Why can't you play basketball in the jungle?

A: Because of all the cheetahs!

BASKETBALL PLAYERS

Basketball teams use five players at a time. They can use any combination of positions they want, but most teams use two guards, two forwards and one center; or two guards and three forwards.

Point guards: These players are usually the shortest and fastest players on the court. Their job is to dribble the ball up the court and pass it to their teammates.

Shooting guards: These players are usually a little bit taller than point guards. They like to shoot the ball from far away, but many shooting guards try to dribble toward the basket for a closer shot.

Small forwards: These medium-sized players are bigger than guards. They sometimes dribble the ball down the court, but mostly they try to get close to the basket to score.

Power forwards: These players are usually more powerful than guards and small forwards. Mostly they try to get close to the goal to score. They also try to grab the ball after the other team misses a shot. This is called rebounding.

Centers: These are usually the biggest players on the court. Centers try to get as close to the basket as possible. Their job is to block the other team from scoring and to get rebounds.

When the game starts, Brianna wants to **score** so bad that she dribbles the ball all the way down the court by herself. She's so fast that she almost makes it all the way to the goal!

But the Bulldogs have some fast players, too. Two of them run toward Brianna. She's trapped! The players poke at the ball and knock it out of Brianna's hands. Then they pass it to one of their teammates, and suddenly the Bulldogs are winning.

"Not again," Brianna thinks.

The referees decide when basketball players step out of bounds, commit fouls or do something against the rules. If the ball goes out of bounds, or if a players steps out of bounds, the other team gets to throw it in. If a player pushes, grabs or gets too rough with a player from another team, the referee can call a foul. And if a player takes too many steps without dribbling the ball, the ref will call traveling, and the other team gets the ball.

"Brianna!" says the Titans' coach. "Don't forget to pass the ball to your teammates!"

"OK, coach," she says. Jayden and Nathan pat Brianna on the back. There is still plenty of time for them to win this game.

CHAPTER 3

Back to Basics

When Brianna and her friends first started playing basketball, they learned how to dribble (bouncing the ball up and down), how to pass (throwing the ball to your teammates) and how to score (shooting the ball into the basket).

In basketball, you aren't allowed to run down the court without dribbling the ball, so they spent a lot of time working on that. During a game, once you stop dribbling you have two choices—pass or shoot. So they spent a lot of time working on those, too.

But in basketball, you can help your team even when you don't have the ball. Jayden and Nathan always try **to get open** when Brianna has the ball. That way if she gets stuck, she can pass it to them and they can try to score.

The National Basketball Association, or NBA, is the most popular professional basketball league in North America. It started with 11 teams back in 1946, but now there are 30. The two best teams play in the NBA Finals at the end of each season, and the winner is the champion.

NBA

JUST JOKING!

Q: Why do basketball players love cookies?

A: Because they can dunk them!

If you make a basket, your team gets points, and the other team takes a turn. That's when it's time to play defense.

When they practice defense, the Titans always work on staying in front of the player with the ball. If a player from the other team gets the ball too close to the basket, then other players from the Titans chip in to help.

If the other team misses their **shot**, one of the taller players from the Titans will jump up and try to get the ball. Sometimes Brianna is so fast, she can get the **rebound** herself!

JUST JOKING!

Q: Why can't basketball players go on vacation?

A: They'd get called for traveling!

When there's a **timeout**, the Titans get together and talk about the things they need to do better.

"Don't forget to help your teammates," their coach might say. "And if you miss your shot, try to get the rebound so you can have another chance to score!"

FUN FACT

When basketball was first invented, players weren't allowed to dribble! The only way to move the ball up the court was to pass it to a teammate. Dribbling didn't become common until the 1950s.

CHAPTER 4

Back to Work

The Titans might be losing against the Bulldogs, but Brianna and her teammates know they still have a chance to win. Their coach always says they have to try their best until the game is over, no matter what the score is.

When Brianna gets the ball, she dribbles up the court as fast as she can. When two players from the Bulldogs try to stop her, she passes it to Jayden!

Jayden is open. Nobody from the Bulldogs is close to him. He thinks about taking the shot … but then he sees Nathan close to the basket!

Jayden passes the ball to Nathan, and Nathan scores! The game is tied!

"Great pass, Brianna," their coach says. "Great pass, Jayden."

JUST JOKING!

Q: What do you call a crazy story about a basketball player?

A: A tall tale!

After the Titans score, it's the Bulldogs' turn. One of their players is dribbling the ball up the court fast. He's almost as fast as Brianna!

Brianna tries her best to keep the other player from scoring. She plays good defense by putting her hands out from her body so she can be ready to block the ball if the other player tries to pass or shoot.

Suddenly, the player from the Bulldogs tries to dribble closer to the basket. Brianna moves with her, and out of nowhere, Jayden is there, too!

They have the other player trapped!

The Bulldogs' player tries to pass the ball to one of his teammates, but he can't pass it over Nathan! Jayden jumps up and grabs the ball, and the Titans have a chance to score again.

FUN FACT

If you try to take a shot and a player from the other team fouls you, you get to shoot free throws. They're called "free" because the other team isn't allowed to try to block the ball. Free throws are only worth one point, but you usually get to shoot more than one.

Once again, Brianna is dribbling the ball up the court. This time, the players from the other team aren't running as fast as her. Brianna tries to dribble all the way and score herself!

But at the last second, a player from the other team steps in front of Brianna. She has nowhere to go.

That's OK. Brianna can always count on her teammates.

Sure enough, she looks up and sees Jayden. After she passes him the ball, Jayden shoots. He scores! The Titans are winning the game!

In most basketball games, your team will score some baskets, and then the other team will score some baskets. And sometimes it goes back and forth like that for the whole game!

The Bulldogs are a really tough team. Their players want to win just like the Titans.

At the end of the game, the Titans have more points. Brianna, Jayden, Nathan and their teammates have won! But they know the Bulldogs tried hard.

After the game, players from both teams shake hands. It was a great game all around. The only bad news is that the season is over.

CHAPTER 5

Good Teammates

Even though basketball season is over, Brianna, Jayden and Nathan still like to hang out.

Sometimes they help each other with their homework. Sometimes they just make each other laugh.

When Brianna needs something off of the top shelf in her room, Jayden grabs it for her. When Jayden needs help carrying something heavy, Nathan is always there to help.

And when Nathan's dog gets off his leash again, Brianna is always there to chase it down.

DID YOU KNOW?

NBA games are divided into four quarters that last 12 minutes each. There's a short break after the first and third quarter. After the second quarter, the teams take a longer break, called halftime. Players can also call a few timeouts during the game if they need an extra break.

Sometimes at school, people make fun of Brianna for being short. That's when Nathan steps in and tells them to leave her alone. All of the kids listen to Nathan when he gets mad.

Sometimes people make fun of Nathan for being so tall. That's when Jayden steps in and reminds everybody to be nice.

And if somebody makes fun of Jayden for not being as fast as Brianna, or not being as strong at Nathan, his two best friends are always there to stick up for him.

Brianna, Jayden and Nathan make a great team, on and off the court. And they can't wait for basketball season to start up again!

The only way to become a good basketball player is to practice. Start by dribbling a ball on any hard surface. You can practice dribbling in your school gym or on the sidewalk in front of your house.

Practice dribbling with both hands. Keep practicing until you can dribble the ball without even looking at it!

Once you get comfortable, practice moving while dribbling. Start slow and keep going faster until you can run and dribble at the same time. Be patient! This takes practice.

You can work on passing with a buddy. Start by pushing the ball to your buddy with both hands. Practice longer passes by moving farther and farther away from your friend.

And, finally, practice shooting. Start close to the goal, then move all around the court. Practice short shots, long shots, and everything in between!

Glossary

center: usually the tallest person on the team; the center usually plays closest to the goal

court: the floor or ground that you play basketball on

forward: medium-sized players who are bigger than guards but not as big as the center

guard: the players who dribble the basketball the most; usually the smallest, fastest players on the team

make baskets: the act of scoring by throwing the ball through the metal hoop

open: [to be open] when a player does not have a defender near him

rebound: catching the ball after another player misses a shot

score: throwing the ball through the metal hoop; see "make baskets"

shot: trying to score by throwing the ball toward the basket

teammates: any of the players on the same team

timeout: a break in the action to rest and talk to your coach

What Did You Learn?

See how much you learned about basketball. Answer *true* or *false* for each statement below. Write your answers on a separate piece of paper.

1 A player gets two points for scoring close to the basket.
True or false?

2 A player gets two points for making a free throw.
True or false?

3 Dribbling is optional. You can run up and down the court without dribbling if you want.
True or false?

4 The center is usually the shortest player on the court.
True or false?

5 NBA baskets are always 10 feet above the floor.
True or false?

For More Information

Books

Burns, Brian; and Mark Dunning. *Skills in Motion: Basketball Step-by-Step.* Rosen Central, 2010.

LeBoutillier, Nate. *Play Basketball Like a Pro* (SI for Kids). Capstone Press, 2010.

Savage, Jeff. *Super Basketball Infographics.* Lerner Publishing, 2015.

Schaller, Bob; and Coach Dave Harnish. *The Everything Kids' Basketball Book.* Adams Media, 2009.

Places

Naismith Memorial Basketball Hall of Fame, Springfield, Massachusetts.

Oracle Arena, Oakland, California. The oldest NBA arena still in use today opened in 1966. Home of the Golden State Warriors.

Web Sites

Jr. NBA and Jr. WNBA
http://www.nba.com/kids

Youth Basketball of America
http://www.yboa.org

Official site of the Hall of Fame
Biographies of over 350 Hall of Fame member players, coaches and teams.
http://www.hoophall.com

Note to educators and parents: Our editors have carefully reviewed these web sites to ensure they are suitable for children. Web sites change frequently, however, and we cannot guarantee that a site's future contents will continue to meet our high standards of quality and educational value. You may wish to preview these sites and closely supervise children whenever they access the Internet.

Index

About the Author

Aaron Derr Aaron Derr is a writer based just outside of Dallas, Texas. He has more than 15 years of experience writing and editing magazines and books for kids of all ages. When he's not reading or writing, Aaron enjoys watching and playing sports, and being a good sport with his wife and two kids.